This book belongs to:

....

For Ma and Pa

First U.S. edition 2010

Library of Congress Cataloging-in-Publication Data is available.
Library of Congress Catalog Card Number pending
ISBN 978-0-7636-4788-9

09 10 11 12 13 CCP 10 9 8 7 6 5 4 3 2 1

Printed in Shenzhen, Guangdong, China

This book was typeset in Centaur MT.
The illustrations were done in watercolor.

TEMPLAR BOOKS
an imprint of Candlewick Press
99 Dover Street
Somerville, Massachusetts 02144
www.candlewick.com

templar books
an imprint of Candlewick Press

THE DJANGO

LEVI PINFOLD

Once, I met a Django.

A what?

A Django. It's like a thing. A sort of it. A kind of cozzler that always seems to find trouble.

It was standing inside our house one day, staring at Papa's banjo.

"Wow, lovely!" it said.

When I went inside, it looked up at me.

"Hello," it said.

"Hello," I said back.

"I like that shiny thing," it said, pointing to the banjo.

"It's nice but it's Papa's and NOBODY is allowed to touch it," I warned.

"Well, imagine that! That's just what I am—a true to life N-O-B-O-D-Y. It's only my middle name," it said as it started to twang the strings.

I said, "Don't!" but it ignored me. Then it started to prance around and sing.

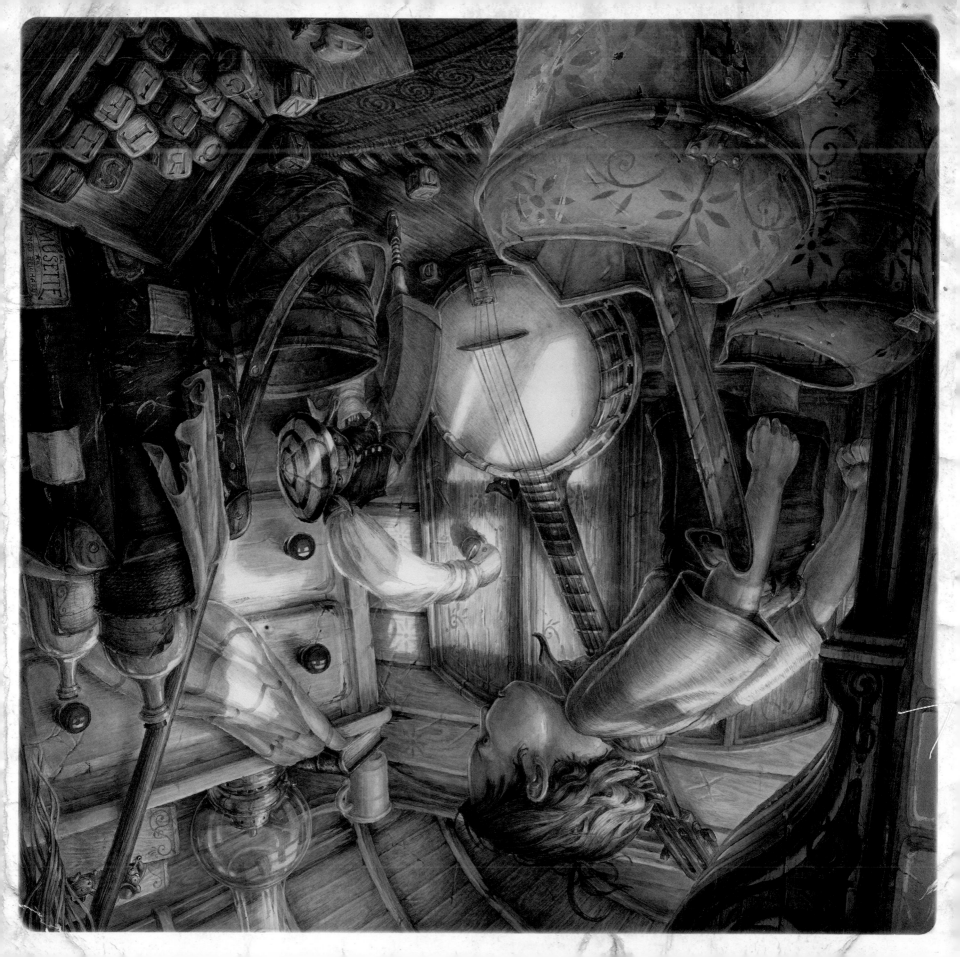

As it sang,

it twanged some more.

And as the strings twanged,

something crackled and crunched.

Then came a *smunch*,

a *swoosh* . . . and *scrunch*.

Then a huge *whack*,

and a massive *SNAP!*

And all of a sudden, Papa's banjo was wrecked.

"*Ho-ho!*" ho-hoed the Django. "That was fun! Have you got another one?"

"Of course not!" I shouted. "Look what you've done!"

In a few moments, Papa arrived, yelling, "What's all this noise? What's the hoo-ha about?"

He saw the smashed-up banjo, then he looked at me.

I said, "It was that *thing* that did it!" pointing to where the Django had been.

"There's NOBODY there!" he yelled.

"I know!" I shouted.

"Well, you're going to bed and you're not having any dinner!" cried Papa.

Oh, that made me mad—I hadn't done a thing!

But from then on the Django began to sneak in.

Papa was still as mad as an ape the next morning, I'll tell you that.

He told me I would have to work to earn the money for a new banjo, starting with fetching some water for Wilfred, the old horse. So off I went, through the trees and down to the waterside. When I got there, I started to fill up my pail.

"Hello," said a voice behind me.

"Not you again! Can't you go away?" I cried.

"Not likely," the Django said. "I'm always around. What are we doing today?"

"Well, *I'm* doing extra chores because of *you*," I snapped, and stomped off with the full water pail.

I went the long way back to the camp, a really screwy path, and I thought I'd lost the horrible little grotsnobbler after that.

I was wrong.

As I carried the pail to Wilfred, that tricksy little Django's face popped out of the bucket. Then, before I could move, it opened its trap, letting out an almighty ear-scrunching yell. A monstrous, massive "GOBBLE-O-GOBBLE-O!" Poor old Wilfred didn't know what to think, so he reared up on his hind legs and ran for it. It took ages to find him and calm him down. And guess who got the blame? ME. Certainly not that thug, that scallywag, the Django!

The next few days were a nightmare. The Django got worse and worse.

Not only was it appearing and disappearing all over the place; it was managing to do other things too. Impossible things.

When we went through town, it did something to my tongue. My words got all jumbled and I said them wrong. Horrible nicknames shot out of my mouth: "Chatty-bum! Goon! Giglet! Slug! Ditch-drone! Voidwit! Fishface! Stinker!"

The Django thought it was tremendously funny. Papa didn't.

The day after that, we moved on.

Papa told me to sit quietly next to him.
As we traveled, all was calm. That was until
I heard that familiar little, *"Ho-bo!"*

In a second, my feet were dancing without
my saying so, and before I could figure out
what was happening I was hopping toward
a farmyard.

That blasted Django was getting into my
legs now, too! I jigged my way into the pigsty,
toe-tapped on the tractor, hoofed it in the
cowfield, and got down with the geese!

What a palaver. Now I had both a cross
farmer and a *fuming* Papa on my hands.

On the third day, it just got silly. My family threw a shindig for Cousin Phillipe's birthday.

Everything was going well, and folks were happy as could be when the band started to play. The problems began when Grandpapa Jaque stood up to dance.

There were suspenders buttoned at bizarre angles, laces in spaghetti tangles, necktie, thumb, and finger mangles, and complex coattail ankle strangles.

Soon everybody was in such a mess that you couldn't tell a shoe from a hat or a moustache from a particularly attractive hairstyle.

Well, you'll never guess who the main suspect was. Go on. It was me! ME!

I got such a scolding for something I hadn't even done.

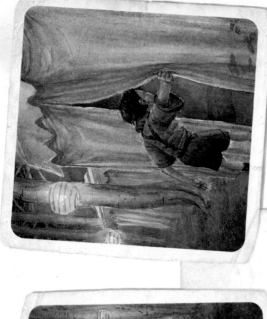

Then I was sent straight to bed.

The Django was already there when I arrived, chuckling. That was it. I exploded.

"You rotten peanut! You squirt! You spoofing little weasel-o! Can't you understand? I don't like your jokes. NOBODY likes your jokes. You don't belong here. GO SOMEWHERE ELSE!"

There was silence. The Django had stopped chuckling.

There was more silence, and then a very small voice came from under the sheets.

"But . . . where would I go?" it asked.

"I don't know! Wherever you were before!" I screeched. "JUST GO AWAY AND LEAVE ME ALONE!"

So it did.

I waited for a "*Ho-bo!*" while I did my chores....

I woke up the next morning expecting something to happen.

I listened for a "GOBBLE-O! GOBBLE-O!" when I fed Wilfred. . . .

By the time supper came, I was ready for a *disaster*. But nothing happened. At all.

At the end of the week, Papa said, "What's wrong, Jean? You're sad as a pike."

"Nothing," I said. "It's just that . . . oh . . . never mind. It's silly."

"Nonsense—you look as if someone's stolen all your marbles. What's making you act like a trodden-on bean, little man?"

"Well . . . you know the Django?"

"Oh," said Papa.

"I . . . I shouted and it went away . . . and . . . I think I kind of liked it, really. I feel bad that I hurt its feelings, but now it won't come back for me to say sorry."

"Oh, dear. That Django's giving you the blues, eh? Well, I think I've got something that might help to fix that," said Papa, pulling a big something wrapped tightly in layers of newspaper out of his bag.

"Go on," said Papa. "Open it—it's yours."

Inside was a lovely, shiny banjo, looking better than new.

"My banjo would have been yours last week, but this one will have to do," said Papa. "Remember, a banjo's much more fun if you can play it, so take care of it."

"I will! I promise!" I said.

I twanged a string, and all of a sudden I felt a little bit better.

"Pluck this one, with your finger on that spot there," said Papa.

I really liked the way it sounded when I did that.

"Wow, thanks!" I said.

Then Papa sat with me for hours and helped me to make a tune with plenty of *Ho-bos* in it. We even made up words.

They went:

Ho, ho, oh, GOBBLE-O
NOBODY's there.
If a Django's the trouble-o,
you'd better beware!

And every time I sing it, a very strange thing
happens. . . .
  I swear I can hear the *tap-tap* of small dancing
shoes and the sound of a small voice *bo-bo-*ing
along with me.
  But when I turn to look, there's nobody there.

What, you don't believe me?
Well, try singing it yourself,
and then you might hear it, too.

THE REAL DJANGO

This book is partly inspired by Django Reinhardt. If you don't know who he was, this is what he looked like:

"What an elegant moustache!" I hear you cry. And you're right. But this man wasn't simply a master of moustache scissors; he was also a very talented jazz musician.

Django Reinhardt was born on January 23, 1910. His mother was a French-speaking Romany, or gypsy, and Django grew up surrounded by this unique culture.

Like little Jean in this book, Django Reinhardt loved music from a very young age. This led him to learn the violin and, as he grew older, the banjo and the guitar. By practicing during every spare moment, Django became so skilled that by the time he was thirteen, he had begun performing onstage. When he was eighteen, he was recorded playing the banjo, and the recording was released as a record.

But just when everything seemed to be going so well for the young musician, a tragic accident happened: a fire began in the caravan he shared with his wife, and Django was badly burned. His right leg was paralyzed, and the third and fourth fingers of his left hand were left almost unusable. It was thought he would never play again.

Then Django surprised everyone: within a year he was walking. But even more startling was his determination to play again. By practicing tirelessly, he taught himself how to play with just two fingers. He was soon performing once more and rapidly turned his bad luck around completely by forming the band La Quintette du Hot Club de France with violinist Stéphane Grappelli. Driven by Django's matchless playing, La Quintette is widely considered to have been one of the greatest European jazz bands in history.